D0429427

About the ONCE UPON AMERICA™ Series

Who is affected by the events of history? Not only the famous and powerful. Individuals from every part of society contribute a *story*—and so weave together *history*. Some of the finest storytellers bring their talents to this series of historical fiction, based on careful research and designed specifically for readers ages 7–11. These are tales of young people growing up in a young, dynamic country. Each ONCE UPON AMERICA volume shapes the reader's understanding of the people who built America and of his or her own role in our unfolding history. For history is a story that we continue to write, with a chapter for each of us beginning, "Once upon America."

Also in the ONCE UPON AMERICA™ Series

A LONG WAY TO GO
by Zibby Oneal

HERO OVER HERE
by Kathleen V. Kudlinski

YOLO COUNTY LIBRARY
226 BUCKEYE STREET
WOODLAND, CA 95695-2600

It's Only Goodbye

BY VIRGINIA T. GROSS

ILLUSTRATED BY LARRY RAYMOND

J
GROSS

VIKING

Thanks to Bernie Gross, whose love for genealogy and
research have kept the story truthful.

VIKING
Published by the Penguin Group
Viking Penguin, a division of Penguin Books USA Inc.,
375 Hudson Street, New York, New York 10014, U.S.A.
Penguin Books Ltd, 27 Wrights Lane, London W8 5TZ, England
Penguin Books Australia Ltd, Ringwood, Victoria, Australia
Penguin Books Canada Ltd, 2801 John Street, Markham Ontario, Canada L3R 1B4
Penguin Books (N.Z.) Ltd, 182–190 Wairau Road, Auckland 10, New Zealand

Penguin Books Ltd. Registered Offices: Harmondsworth, Middlesex, England

First published in 1990 by Viking Penguin, a division of Penguin Books USA Inc.
1 3 5 7 9 10 8 6 4 2
Text copyright © Virginia T. Gross, 1990
Illustrations copyright © Larry Raymond, 1990
All rights reserved

ONCE UPON AMERICA® is a trademark of Viking Penguin, a division of Penguin
Books USA Inc.

Library of Congress Cataloging in Publication Data
Gross, Virginia T.
It's only goodbye / by Virginia T. Gross ; illustrated by Larry Raymond.
p.   cm.—(Once upon America)
Summary: As ten-year-old Umberto and his father are on their way
from Italy to America in 1892, the father is thrown into the ship's
brig and Umberto must fend for himself.
ISBN 0-670-83289-8
[1. Emigration and immigration—Fiction.   2. Italian Americans—
Fiction.]   I. Raymond, Larry, ill.   II. Title.   III. Series.
PZ7.G9043It   1990   [Fic]—dc20   90-32988

Printed in the United States of America
Set in Goudy Old Style

Without limiting the rights under copyright reserved above, no part of this publication
may be reproduced, stored in or introduced into a retrieval system, or transmitted, in any
form or by any means (electronic, mechanical, of both the copyright owner and the above
publisher of this book.

To my grandfather Pietro and to Umberto, his son.

Voices at Midnight

Every boy knows things about his father more private than the skin behind his ears. I know that my father likes the taste of words. He'll use fifteen words to say something another man could say in three. And fancy words taste better than plain.

"Ah, Pietro," folks will say to him. "You are a poet. Your words could melt the ice in a witch's heart."

"Ah, Pietro," Mama often says. "You work your tongue to death. Why don't you rest your poor mouth!"

Mama's teasing always brings the crinkles to Papa's

In the end, Mama would give in. No one could resist Papa, least of all her. But there was still some stretch left in her rope.

"If we had the money, you wouldn't have to work passage. Wait a little longer. We could save the fare and all go together." This sounded good to me, wherever it was we were going.

Not to Papa. He must have knocked the chair over when he jumped up, he was that upset. "If we had the money, Maria, we could have stayed in Italy, our homeland. We came to France because there was no work in Italy. It has taken us ten years to see there is no work in France, either.

"We cannot wait. I must go now. Over there . . . over there is everything!"

"Yes, and you deserve it all, Pietro. But you will be gone many months. If Umberto stayed, it would be company for me. I wouldn't be so alone."

My father's laugh was like a gurgle of warm milk. "You are a sly one, sweet lady, playing with my heartstrings. You'll hardly be alone. Marcelline and Etiènne have opened their home to us. They and their five young ones will be plenty of company for you, as will that little, howling bundle of hunger."

Papa always called Joseph a little bundle of hunger. It's true. His howls could make you forget everything. I was hoping Mama and Papa would not forget to tell me where I was going.

I tried to put the pieces together. Papa and I would go to steerage, where there was very little light or air. Mama and Joseph would come later, after Papa earned some money. It was a long journey, somewhere near the sea—and I'd probably be sick. None of this sounded like fun to me.

Papa was talking again. When his voice got deep, it made me nervous. It was deep now.

"Maria, it is most important that Umberto become thirsty for this adventure. He does not remember Italy. France is all he's ever known. He will be leaving everything and everyone that has made his world.

"He needs to bite into the apple—to feel the juices of excitement in his heart. He needs to meet the Lady and have her swing him from here to there like a monkey on a vine."

I didn't understand any of it, but Papa's words were magic. I could feel those juices in my heart. I could feel myself swinging! Something bothered me, though. What did he mean by leaving everything and everyone?

"I went to Argentina with my brothers when I was but 13," he continued. "I was afraid. I nearly drowned myself with tears when I left my dear mama behind. But the salt winds and ship's roll soon healed my heart. It was the journey that opened me up to the new life ahead."

Ship? Salt winds?

"Maria, it takes much courage to leave all behind. Let go of the boy's hands. Let him reach to the great Lady Liberty. Help him to become a man."

Even for Papa it was a long speech. But it told me everything. Suddenly I knew. I knew it all. I leaned against the icy bedroom wall, hardly able to breathe.

"It's settled then?" Mama said at last.

"Yes," said Papa. "The *Chateau LaFite* is in Bordeaux Harbor. It leaves at month's end. Your husband and son will be aboard."

The quilt was all churned under me when I fell back on the bed. The secret lumped inside me. I was going to *America!* It was March 3, 1892.

Fog and Fire

When I said goodbye to Mama, fog sat upon the land and sadness sat upon my heart.

"Umberto, don't look so glum," said Mama. "You are on your way to see Lady Liberty."

Mama looked pretty glum herself. Besides, I didn't care about some other lady. Mama was good enough for me.

"Hold Joseph," she said, handing the baby to Papa. "I have something to give Umberto."

She reached under her apron to the dress pocket

where treats were kept. Instead of a sweet, she pulled out a soft cloth bag wrapped with leather strings.

"What is it, Mama?" I asked.

Papa looked amazed. "Maria, are you sure—?"

Mama gave Papa a look I had never seen before. It said, "Don't dare open your mouth about this!" Papa was speechless, but I don't know if it was because of the package or the look.

"This belonged to my father, your grandfather. He wanted you to have it one day when you were a man."

She held my chin in her hands. Her smile was sadder than tears. "That day is coming soon, I think. Meanwhile, you keep this with you, and let it remind you of me."

The package was heavy. When I unwrapped it, even my own tears could not keep me from being dazzled by the shine of the gold watchcase. The lid snapped open to show a small diamond above each number. On the face were the initials, *U.S.*—Umberto Santoro, my grandfather's name, and mine. I am Umberto Santoro Ameliori.

"Mama," I croaked, "I will keep it forever." Little did I know what a short time it would be before my promise was broken!

Riding all day in a two-wheeled cart can take your mind off "goodbye." It's a good thing, because my

mama's goodbye left me as washed away as the moon in daylight.

Papa had arranged for us to ride with a farmer who was bringing chickens to his sister in Bordeaux. The trip would take four days.

"Why can't we sail from Marseilles, Papa?" I wanted to know.

"Because the mighty Captain Leveque, whom you will meet and for whom I will work, sails from Bordeaux." And that was that!

We left in the thick fog. Papa and the farmer, Gabriel, shared the driver's seat. I shared the wagon with satchels and a crate of chickens.

The weight of the luggage made the wagon slant backward. That made me slide into the chickens and that made the chickens very nervous. When I tried using the crate as a backrest, the chickens pecked my ears. When the chickens did what chickens do, it smelled terrible.

A lot of sliding, pecking, and smelling went on before we reached the village where we'd spend the night. My body was so sore I could hardly feel the ache in my heart.

"This place is not fancy," said our driver, "but it is the only inn for another 40 miles. The forests are too dangerous after dark." He ran his finger across his throat in case we didn't understand what he meant.

I helped him bring the chickens to a small barn

behind the inn. The driver and the innkeeper counted them and signed a paper saying there were 11.

Meanwhile, Papa brought our bags inside and paid for one room for the three of us. That was the deal we had made with the farmer. We paid for his bed in trade for a ride.

As we sat down to supper, I noticed two men sitting nearby. The innkeeper's wife was serving them stew. They were chewing hard bread and laughing at some joke.

During our meal, Gabriel and Papa included me in the conversation. I felt like the man I was soon to be, sharing food and talk in this way. It wasn't long before I reached into my shirt and brought out the gold watch. I wanted Gabriel to know that my mother thought I was a man also.

Papa frowned, but didn't say anything. Gabriel thought the watch was splendid. He remarked about the diamonds and held it up to the fire where they caught the light.

It had become quiet in the room and I thought the other two men had left. I glanced their way, but they were busy eating their custard. I took the watch back and got ready to enjoy my own sweet dessert.

Nothing could feel better than that lumpy mattress in the bed I later shared with my father and Gabriel. Our room was a small attic at the top of the stairs, with only enough space for the bed. There would be no baths this night, so we slept in our clothes.

How long I'd been asleep, I don't know, when the bedroom door burst open and someone yelled, "Fire!" I was grabbed by strong arms and carried to the hall. The smell of smoke choked me.

"I've got the boy," said an unfamiliar voice. "Grab your bags! You can still make it down the stairs."

I was bumped against the wall and hurried past the landing where yellow flames were leaping from inside a barrel. I saw the innkeeper and his wife carrying buckets of water.

The stranger rushed me to the front door. "Papa!" I yelled. I was afraid he might not make it outside in time. At that instant, my rescuer tripped and we both went crashing and rolling off the front porch.

The stranger was up like lightning. "Are you hurt?" he asked, brushing me off. We had fallen into soft grass. My head was spinning, but I was all right.

"I'm not hurt," I answered. "But where is Papa?"

"There he is now," said the man. He turned my head toward the house. Papa stood in the doorway, looking for me. The fire seemed to be out.

"Here I am, Papa," I called, running to him. "This man helped me." I turned to the man. But he had disappeared into the darkness. It didn't matter. Papa

was fine. So was Gabriel. The innkeeper invited us to have hot wine. By now I was wide awake. Hot wine would help.

It wouldn't be until the next day that I'd remember how calm the innkeeper seemed, serving our wine, as if this kind of thing happened all the time. And it wouldn't be until the next day that I'd realize my grandfather's watch was gone.

City of Rain

The rains of southern France are mean in late March. We all sat in our private gloom, Gabriel, the chickens, and I.

We had arrived in Bordeaux at noon. My father had us drive to the old section so he could shop for supplies. We would be allowed a small kerosene stove in our quarters, with enough kerosene for two weeks. Papa wanted to buy a round of salt cheese and some dried peas.

Seaport merchants also sold bottles of fresh drinking water to passengers who felt the ship's supply would

not be enough. Papa often said that if everyone drank a gallon of good clean water every day, half the world's troubles would be washed away. I felt I was carrying all the world's troubles in my lap, so I was ready to start on my gallon at once!

The rains had begun as we turned north into the valley of the Garrone. Papa and Gabriel had shared a huge umbrella. The chickens and I shared a canvas tarp. That didn't keep us dry, but it did keep us from drowning.

We drove without stopping. For miles, nothing could be seen except gray clouds and hillsides covered with budding grapevines. After two days, I was sure that the world produced nothing but rain and grapes.

Now Gabriel and I sat under the big umbrella, watching the run-down shops and narrow streets for a sign of Papa. Where was he? My mood was as dark as the day.

While we waited in the rain, my mind turned to my mother. Her heart would break when she learned what had happened to the watch. For four days, I had been swallowing anger, anger with everyone. When Papa joined us at last, loaded with bundles and soaking wet, I could not look at him.

At the waterfront, we found the pier where the *Chateau LaFite* was docked. "Wait here," said Papa. "I will find Captain Leveque and see about boarding." Wait again!

Papa disappeared among the pilings, talking to some sailors, laughing and shaking their hands. At least *he* was having a good time.

The black-and-red hull of the ship took up most of the sky, as I looked up at it from below. Its three masts had their sails furled tight. Papa said they would be used only if the steam failed. No steam was coming out of the ship's funnel now, but we wouldn't be sailing until morning.

It wasn't long before Papa returned. "I've just met the captain," he said cheerfully. "We can board soon. Umberto, come with me and see how things are done in the real world." Papa was in high spirits. He had forgotten all about the watch.

"I'll be right back, Gabriel."

"I'll be right here," Gabriel answered. And I knew he would. After sharing the trickery at the inn that first night, we had trusted no one but each other. Gabriel had become our friend.

We walked through crowds of people to a big building. There were no rooms inside, only rows of long tables. Over each table was the name of a ship. When we found *Chateau LaFite*, we took our place in line.

Families and bundles and small pushcarts were everywhere. Everyone seemed to be talking at once, with a muddle of sounds. Because Mama and Papa spoke Italian, I understood it well. And going to school

in France I knew French, also. But the other languages sounded like crazy talk.

Up ahead was a family with three children, two girls and a boy. The boy's eyes were large and sad and they were staring at me. When our eyes met, he looked quickly away.

At last it was our turn. Papa stepped up to the table. The officer in charge had a face like bread dough. "Your papers?" he said, without looking up. It was easy to see that going to America was not as exciting for him as it was for my father.

The man asked Papa the most embarrassing questions. No, we were not criminals. No, we were not insane, although I was beginning to believe it was possible. No, we had no diseases that were catching. Yes, we planned to work in America. Yes, we had our $40.00. Yes, relatives would take us in. Papa had cousins in Rochester, New York.

The officer stamped our papers. "You will be in steerage." Papa had told me all about steerage. The more I heard, the less I liked.

"You are not to be above decks or mingle with the first-class passengers for any reason," continued the man. He sounded annoyed.

"I will be working among the first-class passengers," said Papa smoothly. He was tickled to tell the dough-faced man that he would be above decks one way or another. With that, he took my arm and we walked away. Papa was whistling.

As we walked out into the rain, I noticed the boy with the sad eyes watching us.

Gabriel was waiting, just as he promised. Before long, we had said yet another goodbye. "Umberto," said Papa gently. "It is just we two now."

I followed him up the swaying gangplank to the ship. The height of it made me dizzy. I stepped on deck and felt the lift of the water so far below.

"Frank, this is my son, Umberto." Already Papa had made a friend!

The man held out his hand, covered with freckles and curly red hairs. "Welcome aboard, matey," he smiled.

We found our living space in steerage. Papa had been right. There was very little air. The only light came from a few kerosene lamps and from tiny portholes in every other section.

Each section was called a compartment, one compartment to a family. The walls did not go all the way to the ceiling. The doorways had no doors. For two weeks we'd know who fought, who cried, and who snored!

I looked for our beds and saw a bunk nailed into the wall. Just one. It looked big enough for a person and a half. Papa was watching me. He smiled. "We'll manage," he promised. "You're no wider than a broom." I didn't smile.

24

I noticed the family with the sad-eyed boy three compartments away from ours. There were three bunks stacked in that section. When the boy saw me, he looked down.

That night as I lay in the dark, I began to think of Mama. I sighed.

"What is it, Umberto?"

Papa was lying so close it must be he could hear me thinking!

"I miss Mama," I said, still a little angry with him for feeling excited and happy.

"Ah, yes," he said. "But goodbye is not forever. It's only goodbye. Mama will be with us soon."

"But the watch!"

"We can do nothing about that. Mama is in your heart. You don't need a watch to remind you."

"It had my initials on it."

"Only two of them. When I earn enough money, I'll get you another watch with all your initials. And do you know what they'll say?"

"What?"

"U.S.A. The same initials as our new country."

I smiled in the dark. Who could stay angry with Papa!

"I still miss Mama," I said after a while.

"I know," he said softly. He sighed. He missed her, too. I knew, because I could hear what he was thinking.

Papa's Rage

When I heard the baby crying, I thought it was Joseph, but Joseph was with Mama, miles away. Only Papa lay sleeping next to me.

The gray dawn filled our space with shadows. I could feel the growl of the engines shivering through the ship.

"Papa! Wake up. We're leaving!"

My father popped out of our bunk and headed for the washbowl. "Hurry, Umberto! Hurry!"

I hurried, splashing cold water on my face and stepping into my britches. No one else, except the baby and its mother, was awake. I could barely keep up with Papa as he rushed toward the hatchway which led to the upper decks.

We came out into the morning. The cold wrapped itself around my neck.

Papa led me along the cabin toward the railing. No one on shore bothered to look at the ship as it nosed into the channel. I whispered a quiet farewell to France, the only homeland I'd known. By locking my teeth together, I managed not to cry.

Papa was hearing me think, even though we were not in steerage. "My son," he said, speaking Italian instead of French, "now we look ahead. In our new land, we will greet Lady Liberty. It is very important to greet her well. It is good luck."

We pressed our hands to each other's, promising that we would greet Lady Liberty well—for luck.

"What are you doing up here?" The loud voice made us jump.

"I am preparing for work, sir," said Papa, always one step ahead of any surprise. "I was hoping to have my son meet you. Allow me to present Umberto Santoro Ameliori. Umberto, Captain Leveque."

The man was tall, but not as tall as Papa. When he looked at my father, he had to look up. "Report to your duties, and do not have the boy above decks again."

"Yes, sir," said Papa, grinning down at him. "Come, Umberto, we have work to do."

My father brought me to a long, narrow room, busy with people, pots, and pans. I'd never seen a kitchen like this before. "This is the galley," said Papa, proud to talk like a sailor.

All that day, I followed Papa from galley to dining room and back again. The names on the ship's passenger list added up to 1300. Most of these people, about 1200, travelled like us, in steerage. The rest ate on white tablecloths and used fine silver. These were the first-class passengers. Papa poured their wine and served their soup.

Gawain, the cook, was a young man who liked to laugh. He and Papa were friends at once. They let me stay in the galley and even taught me to make myself useful in small ways.

That night, we were so tired that Papa and I fell asleep on the way to our pillows. In the morning, the ship was pitching and rolling and making it hard to stand up. Papa chuckled.

"Look out the porthole, and tell me what you see," he said. I went to the porthole.

"I see nothing!" I exclaimed. And that's all there was. Nothing! In the night, we had left land behind.

I wasn't in the galley three minutes when my stomach went to war with my head. By mid-morning, Gawain and his helpers were laughing and helping me to the slop bowl each time it was necessary. It took three days before I was able to keep my biscuits where they belonged. Papa never got seasick at all. Something worse was in store for him.

The morning of the fourth day started like any other, but for Papa and me it would end in disaster.

Breakfast was being served. Papa left the galley with a full pot of coffee. He went to a table where a round, middle-aged man was sitting. He began to pour the man's coffee. At that moment, the ship gave a lurch and the boiling hot coffee landed on the man's hand.

"I'm so sorry, sir!" cried Papa. He reached for a napkin.

"Why didn't you watch what you were doing!" yelled the man.

"It was an accident, sir," Papa protested.

"Accidents happen when numbskulls try to do a man's work!"

I don't think Papa knew what a numbskull was, but I could see he didn't like the man's attitude. It's too bad for the man that he didn't notice.

"But, sir," Papa tried again. "The ship, she . . ."

The man shouted, "Don't you talk back to me, you clumsy dago!"

Now, I have seen Papa annoyed, and I have seen him angry, but until this day I had never seen his rage. He threw the coffeepot onto the table. Dragging the man from his chair, he screamed into his face, "Your insult shames the proud land of my birth. Nobody, sir,

nobody insults my homeland!" With the strength of two bulls, he slammed his fists into the man's face. The man fell down.

"Papa!" I screamed. Passengers screamed. Gawain and his helpers rushed from the galley to pull my father away. A porter ran for the captain. I was nailed to the floor with horror.

The captain roared into the dining room. "Ameliori," he barked, "I knew you'd be trouble. From this moment, you are no longer a passenger or a worker. You are a prisoner! Take him to the brig and lock him up!"

"But my son!" cried Papa, looking for me, as he was pulled out of the dining room by two young sailors.

Captain Leveque's glance touched me briefly. He looked away. I was no concern of his. He had a ship to run. "Back to your duties," he ordered the crew. He, himself, tended to the man on the floor.

Alone at Sea

The pillow was soaking from my sobs. This was too much. Too much shame and anger and loneliness and fear. I took turns crying first because of one and then because of the other.

How long the sad-eyed boy was standing there, I don't know.

"What do you want? Can't you do anything but look at me?" I choked.

"I want to help, but I do not know French," he said in Italian. So that's why he never spoke.

"I speak Italian, also."

He smiled with relief. "I am Georgio. We are travelling to America."

"Of course," I said. "Where else? But why did you not sail from Italy?"

"My father looked for work in France. There was none. He is a roofer. Now we try America. Pittsburgh. There is much building there."

I invited him to sit on the bunk with me. Before long, I had shared my father's story. "He's locked up in the brig. No one will let me near him," I finished. I could say no more. Tears got in the way. I couldn't help it.

"What will you do now? You cannot stay by yourself."

"I'm hardly by myself," I snorted, smelling the cooking from the other compartments. Then I realized that none of that food was for me. "I'll stay here, I guess." I wondered what Papa would be eating.

"I'll be right back." Georgio spun out of the room. After a very long time, a man came to the doorway.

"Umberto Ameliori," he said. "The captain wants to see you." It was Georgio's father.

The captain's quarters were one big room shaped like a U. There were real windows all around. At the far end was a spiral stairway that led up to the bridge. Captain Leveque sat at a desk.

"Young man," he started, without time for "hello." "I didn't want to hire your father for this voyage, but

I was told to do it by the ship's owner. I certainly didn't want you, but you are here."

I said nothing. I didn't want to be here either.

"What can you do?"

"What do you mean, sir?"

"I mean, your father and you are not paying passengers! Your father was working for his passage. Now he is in jail. He is getting a free ride! But *you* will not." His voice got louder with every word. "What can you do?"

"I am ten years old, sir," I said, "and strong and tall. I can do anything."

He looked at me for a minute, then said quietly, "You will work for me. I had to send my ship's boy to take your father's place in the dining room. You will take over his chores. You are to report here each day at dawn. You will remain here until sundown. You will be fed in the galley. You must give the purser in charge the food rations you brought with you. There will be no nonsense and you will work hard. Do you understand me?"

"Yes, sir."

"Good. You may go."

"Thank you, sir."

One thing had not been settled. Although the man scared me and made me angry, I had to ask. At the door, I stopped.

"Captain Leveque, sir?"

"What is it?"

"May I see my father?"

"Absolutely not! And if I find you've disobeyed me, you will be made to stay in your quarters and will owe me your passage in gold!"

I could see the man meant business. "Yes, sir," I said, and left.

Below decks, Georgio was sitting on my bunk, waiting. "My father says I can stay with you at night so you won't feel so alone."

For the first time that day, something good had happened. My heart warmed. "Thank you, Georgio."

He laughed. "It's a favor to us, too. More room!"

I told him all about my visit to the captain. "Georgio," I said. "I've *got* to see my father. Will you help me?"

He opened his mouth to speak, but said nothing.

"It's all right, Georgio. You are doing enough. I understand. No need for all of us to be in trouble."

"When?"

I smiled. "Soon. Maybe tomorrow night." I waited.

"I'll help you," he said at last. "There's nothing else to do, anyway."

I knew he was scared to death. So was I. But he was brave and I was stubborn. We'd make it work.

That night, I fell asleep praying for Mama and Papa, missing them both, feeling so alone. But sleeping beside me, in the middle of the Atlantic Ocean, was my new friend. We moved on toward America.

Sneaking Passage

All next day, my mind played with plans for seeing Papa. The captain kept me busy, polishing this and buffing that. At sundown, when I left for the galley, I was tired.

Gawain's good food and good spirits gave me energy. I left the galley quickly. I had a discovery I needed to share with Georgio.

"There is a map of the ship on the captain's wall," I told him. "It shows every passageway and room. I have studied it and know exactly where to locate the brig."

"Umberto! Good work. Maybe in America you will be a great detective."

We both laughed and settled in to wait for things to quiet down. We would start out when everyone was asleep. Someone had a concertina and was playing French songs. I felt like singing and taught two songs to Georgio. Farther away, some men were playing cards for money. It was noisy and maybe not all in fun.

Georgio and I began to talk of America. We would land in eight days. Papa and I would take a train to Rochester, about 400 miles inland. In the old country, Papa was a shoemaker, but he thought having a grocery store on Main Street, America, might be nice.

We talked about school and what it would be like not to know the language and how it would be not to have any friends. When I thought of friends, I realized I'd be saying goodbye—again.

As we talked, the ship began to sway and creak more than usual. Suddenly a midshipman was at the opening above the passageway.

"We have sailed into blowing winds. All lamps out, please." Everyone groaned. "Better dark than fire," said the midshipman. "It should last only until morning."

"Papa! Georgio, we won't be able to go!" If I didn't see Papa soon, I might die of hunger for him. But we had no choice. We spent the rest of the night in pitch darkness, dreaming and talking of America.

Each of the next two nights, it stormed. My heart reached out to Papa, all alone in the brig. At last, three nights later, the sea calmed and Georgio and I laid our plans.

Everyone was quiet, except for the cardplayers who continued their game late into each night. I knew that if Papa were here, his laugh would be the loudest. We walked past the men. No one noticed us.

I carried the lamp and led the way. We would have to travel the whole length of the ship. Our shadows leaped at us and made us jump.

"Are you scared, Georgio?" I whispered.

"No," he lied.

We went up and down ladders, silent as ghosts haunting the great ship. The engines churned and bilge water sloshed, sometimes near, sometimes far.

At last we came to a closed door. "This is it, Georgio. This is the brig." In minutes, I'd be with Papa. I put my hand on the latch, but just as I touched it, the hatch opened quickly from the other side! I gasped as a huge hand reached forward. Even in the lamplight, I could see the freckles and the red hairs.

"What have we here?" said a thick, familiar voice. It was Frank! He was as surprised to see us as we were to see him.

"You two should be back in your bunk, fast asleep!" he said gruffly. "What are you doing here?"

I managed to explain how I missed Papa and simply had to see him.

"Impossible! I've just come from your father. He is fine. You two, on the other hand, are in deep trouble."

"Please, sir, could you take us to my father? Just for a minute?"

"No, lad, I can't. Rules are rules and on shipboard we obey them. Now, I'm going to take you back to where you came from and I want no fuss."

The card game was still going on as the three of us walked by. No one paid any attention.

I climbed into bed. I wanted to thank Georgio, but I couldn't speak without crying. Suddenly a thought bolted through me. I sat up.

"What is it?"

"Georgio, if Papa doesn't get out of jail, he won't be on deck to greet Lady Liberty. Papa told me you must greet your new land, for luck."

I made up my mind to speak with the captain, even if he threw me overboard. There were only a few days left.

The Day Before Tomorrow

We had been at sea for twelve nights. Most of those nights I had shared my bunk with Georgio. He was my guest, so I let him sleep on the outside. We talked as much as we slept. The bunk was big enough for the two of us and all our dreams and plans and secrets.

On the morning before we were to land, I climbed carefully over Georgio. This *had* to be the day I talked to Captain Leveque.

"Umberto?"

"What is it?"

"Here. Wear this."

Georgio, half-asleep, took a gold chain from around his neck. It held a medal of the Virgin Mary. I remembered the last valuable thing I had been given. "No," I said.

"Take it, please, Umberto. Wear it for luck when you talk to the captain. You can give it back when you've freed your father from jail."

"Well . . . as long as I'll be giving it back. All right, then. Thank you, Georgio. Go back to sleep."

I put the chain around my neck and left for the captain's cabin. I made his bunk, fluffed his pillows, and shook the rugs. There was one good thing about working for Captain Leveque. I didn't have to spend the long days in steerage. Going back down, after having been in fresh sea air, brought me close to losing my dinner each night. The smell!

I hadn't spoken to the captain since the day Papa went to jail. My voice surprised us both.

"Sir?"

"Yes?"

"Tomorrow we will be in New York Harbor."

"I know that!" This was not going well.

"My father, sir, when will he be free?"

The captain's face tightened. His lips barely moved as he spoke. "Your father does nothing but make trouble. He will remain locked up until every passenger is off this ship!"

43

My heart sank. "No, sir. You can't!"

"What?"

"I mean, sir, he must see the Statue of Liberty. He *must.*" The captain stared at me.

I started again, but my voice was shaking. This man would never understand my father's feeling about coming to America. I tried anyway. "Papa told me that we must greet our new land . . . that we must greet Lady Liberty—for luck."

"Your father has run out of luck."

"He doesn't *mean* luck," I protested. "He means we are doing something grand and—and that we must be part of it from the start—from the very start—from the first instant or—or it just won't be right. My father is a poet!" I was almost screaming, but I didn't care.

"Your father is a very foolish man!" The captain was almost screaming, too. "Your father is locked up because he started a fight on board ship. That is where he will stay. Now step outside and pull yourself together. Then come back in and get to work."

"Y-yes, sir." I turned and ran. Outside, the wind pinched the tears off my face. I rubbed my eyes on my sleeve and looked at the horizon. Were my eyes playing tricks or was something there? Then I heard the voice from the bridge—words I thought I'd never hear.

"Land, ho! Land, ho!"

The captain was on the bridge looking through a

telescope. The ship's whistle shook the sky with a long blast, then another.

"Oh, Papa!" I couldn't stop my tears. Passengers began to swarm on deck. All passengers except those in steerage and those in jail. My heart was breaking.

For the rest of the day, I did my duties like a puppet, except that puppets don't cry. I cried more on this trip than ever in my whole life. Is this what it took to become a man?

Georgio wanted to know what the land looked like. Steerage passengers wouldn't be allowed on deck until the last day.

"There's nothing to see," I told him. "A little gray on the horizon, that's all." He helped me begin to pack our things.

Little by little, the gray on the horizon changed to blue and became bigger. Tomorrow we'd see Lady Liberty.

"I'll greet her for you, Papa," I promised.

Lady Liberty,
Lady Luck

Papa is a wizard at playing cards. When he first taught me to play, he taught me something else. "Umberto," he said, "you must learn to wait for luck. Luck is in the cards for everyone. Your turn will come."

My turn came this morning, and what a turn it was! Only I wasn't playing cards.

I had finished my chores in the captain's cabin. I was free to go below to help passengers get their belongings on deck.

People who had not seen daylight for two weeks stumbled up the ladders. At the sight of land and the

feel of April sun, men and women burst into tears. I felt right at home with crying.

Georgio and I had been working side by side. Together we were lugging people and bundles through the hatchway, when someone yelled, "There she is!"

Everyone stopped and looked forward. In the distance, against blue shadows, was the outline of Lady Liberty, no bigger than a needle. We were still far away. The ship became deathly quiet. Only the hissing water and the thumping engines let us know we had not turned to stone.

It was more hushed than being at Holy Mass, and I guessed most people were praying. We stood there, in silence, for half an hour while the Lady came nearer and nearer. The tugboats had come to meet us and were steering us toward the harbor.

I'm not sure what called my attention to the fuss behind me. It started with little stirrings and then bigger noises. "Let me through. Let me through here, please." It was a familiar voice. It was . . .

"*Papa!*"

Head and shoulders above everyone, he was pushing toward me.

"*Papa!*" I screamed again, and then I was being crushed into his arms.

Papa's story had travelled among all the families below decks. Every one of them agreed that had someone insulted their homeland, they would have done the same thing.

When I turned to the crowd and said, "This is my papa. He's free!" a cheer went up, gently at first, then louder and louder until everyone on deck joined in. Never before or since has Lady Liberty been greeted in such a way as when the steamer *Chateau LaFite* passed under her torch.

As I hugged my father again and again, I noticed two things over his shoulder. The sweet smile on Lady Liberty's face as she towered above us, and the soft smile on Captain Leveque's as he watched us from the bridge.

In Newport News, Virginia, there is a place where you can grab the magic of adventure on the high seas. At the Mariner's Museum, you'll find the history of ships and shipping from past to present. Books, ship logs, insurance documents, diaries and memoirs, newspaper accounts and personal letters—all are here for the looking.

In the summer of 1988, my husband and I spent hours at the museum gathering information about *Chateau LaFite*. It was important to me, you see, because this ship brought my father and his father to America. The book you've just read is based on their true adventure. Such a good story had to be told.

At the museum, we learned that *Chateau LaFite* was a small ship. It was probably used for shipping wine, as it was owned by the Bordeaux Line, nicknamed "The Wine Line." It was about as long as a football field and as wide as a good-sized house. To make more money, it also carried passengers—as many as 1200 in steerage and 50 in first class.

Passengers in steerage had few comforts. Although the coming of steam power shortened the ocean crossing from 40 to 14 days, it was a long time to live below deck. People grew weary. Sometimes tempers got short. The captain of the ship had to keep perfect order. He acted as policeman and judge. If trouble started, punishment was swift. The brig was always ready.

We'll never know what really happened on that ship in February of 1889, the year my father, then six years old, came to America. We do know that his father was put in the brig for hitting a passenger who called him a name while he was serving hot soup or coffee. And we know that my father was looked after by the captain, listed as C. Oliver. The story on these pages comes from scouting out information in the National Archives in Washington, D.C., and from reading many books about immigration, ships, and shipping at the turn of the century. It also comes from my own imagination and from my many years of being with children, as a mother and as a teacher.

Was there really a Georgio? Perhaps. Umberto? Yes. And there really was a Pietro, who died long before I was born. How lucky for me to be able to bring them to life in this, my first book.

—V.T.G.

DA OCT 1 0 1995